Spotter's Guide to
HORSES &
PONIES

Joanna Spector

Illustrated by David Wright,
Elaine Keenan & Malcolm McGregor

with additional illustrations by
Ed Roberts and Andy Martin

Special Consultant
Gerard A. Caserto
American Horse Shows Association, New York

Contents

Edited by Tim Dowley and
Felicity Mansfield

First published in 1979 by
Usborne Publishing Limited,
Usborne House
83-85 Saffron Hill
London EC1N 8RT
England

Printed in Great Britain

How to use this book

This book is an identification guide to breeds of horses and ponies from all over the world. Take it with you when you go to shows, riding stables, races or any place that you might see horses.

The breeds are arranged with ponies first, followed by riding horses, harness horses and work horses.

Next to each picture is a short description of the breed, telling you where the breed comes from, what kind of work it does, the colours it can be, and its height. It also points out any special details about the breed.

Some of the colours have unusual names. You can look them up on page 7. If there are any other words you don't understand, look them up in the glossary on page 58, or find them on the diagram showing the parts of a horse on page 49.

Checklist

There is a small blank circle next to each description. When you see a breed, make a mark in the circle. You will be able to find some of the breeds in Britain and North America. Others live either in particular areas of the country, or in other countries, so they will be harder to find. Others are very rare indeed; you will probably see them only in zoos. The checklist at the end of the book enables you to mark when and where you saw each breed. You can mark off very rare breeds if you see them in a film or on television.

Height

The height of horses and ponies is measured in hands, from the ground to the top of the withers. One hand equals 4 inches (10 centimetres). If the description says that a horse is 15.2 hh, for example, it means that the horse is 15 hands and 2 inches high (hh means "hands high"). Ponies are usually less than 14.2 hh.

Withers

Height is measured in hands

Mark off each horse or pony when you have seen it

How horses began

Arab horse

Exmoor pony

The first horse looked rather like a deer. It lived in forests and woodlands, 50 million years ago. Gradually, different types of horses began to appear. They all became fast and sure-footed, because they had to be able to run away from their enemies.

All the breeds we know today are descended from two ancient types of horses – the southern type, from the hot deserts of North Africa and southern Asia, and the northern type, from cold, hilly or mountainous parts of Europe and Asia.

The southern type had a fine, silky coat and light bones. It could run fast and survive on small amounts of food. It was similar to the Arab horse of today. The northern type had a thick, rough coat and sturdy legs. It lived off poor, scrubby grass and bushes. This type was similar to breeds like the Przewalski and Exmoor of today. Several thousand years ago, in Europe, man began to control the development of horses like these. There are now about 200 different breeds of horses and ponies.

Wild Horses

The only truly wild breed left in the world is the Przewalski, from the Gobi Desert in Mongolia, where some still live in wild herds.

The Przewalski

How horses are used

To begin with, horses were hunted for food. Later on they were bred to do all sorts of work. Harness horses, for example, pull light carts and carriages, while work horses are used for ploughing and hauling (pulling heavy carts and wagons). Today, people ride mostly for pleasure or sport, although some horses still work on farms, especially in eastern Europe.

Heavy work horse pulling a plough

▼ In the 19th century, three Arab stallions were crossed with English hunters to produce the Thoroughbred, the finest riding horse ever bred. It gets its qualities of speed, good looks and endurance from the Arab.

Throroughbred racehorses

Looking at horses

At first, it is difficult to tell what breed a horse or pony is, but after a while, it becomes easier. Here are some clues to help you:

Welsh pony

Highland pony

If the horse carries its tail high and has a dished profile (a face that curves in), it probably has some Arab blood. It may be an Anglo-Arab, or even a Welsh pony.

If it is small and sturdy, with a long, rough coat, it is probably a mountain or moorland pony – perhaps a Highland or Dartmoor pony.

Thoroughbred

Percheron

If the horse is tall, with long legs, a fine skin and coat, and a light build, it is probably a Thoroughbred.

If it is big, heavy and slow, with feather (long hairs) around its fetlocks, it is probably a heavy horse, like a Percheron or a Shire.

Where to look
Many of the horses you see are likely to be cross-bred. It can be fun trying to guess which different breeds their ancestors were. Look for pure-bred horses and ponies at:
- Horse shows, where there are classes for various breeds.
- Stud farms, where horses are bred. (This is probably the best place to find pure-breeds.)
- The breed's natural surroundings. For example, hills and moors in Britain, lowlands in France and Belgium, mountains in Austria.
- Racing stables or racetracks (these are the best places to see Thoroughbreds).
- Riding stables. At the Spanish Riding School in Vienna, for example, you will see only Lipizzaners.

Ask at your nearest riding school if any of their horses or ponies are pure-bred.

Colours and markings

Most breeds are the common colours – bay, brown, chestnut and grey. Some are always a particular colour. For example, the Fjord pony is always dun.

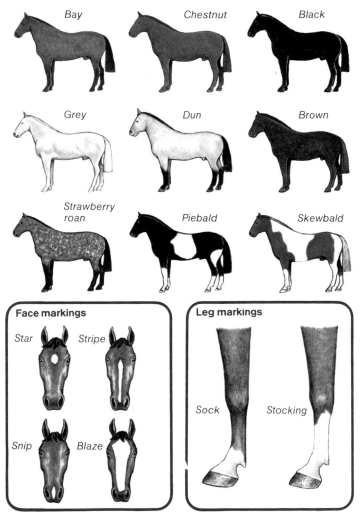

Bay

Chestnut

Black

Grey

Dun

Brown

Strawberry roan

Piebald

Skewbald

Face markings

Star

Stripe

Snip

Blaze

Leg markings

Sock

Stocking

Ponies

Thick mane
and tail

Highland ▶
Comes from the Scottish
Highlands. Largest British
pony. Once used as a
pack pony. Popular for
driving and trekking.
Usually grey or dun; can
be black or
chestnut. Long
winter coat.
Up to 14.2 hh.

Short, strong
neck

◀ Shetland
Smallest British pony.
Once used to carry peat.
Popular as pet for riding
and driving. Usually black,
brown or chestnut. Can be
piebald or
skewbald.
About 9.2 hh.

Dale ▶

Comes from the Pennine hills, in northern England. Was used as a pack pony; now used in harness and on farms. Slightly bigger and heavier than the Fell pony. Usually dark brown or black. May have white markings. Up to 14 hh.

Lots of feather

◀ Fell

Comes from higher regions of the western Pennines. Still used by farmers for herding cattle and sheep. Usually black, sometimes brown or bay. No white markings. About 14 hh.

Light-coloured muzzle

Rough, springy coat

Exmoor ▶

Oldest breed in Britain. Several herds still live half wild on Exmoor, in southwest England. Hardy and strong willed. Good riding ponies for children. Bay or brown with light coloured underside. Up to 12.3 hh.

Small, pretty head

◀ Dartmoor

Lives half wild on Dartmoor, southwest England. Hardy and sure footed. Excellent children's riding pony. Intelligent and elegant. Bay, black or brown. Up to 12 hh.

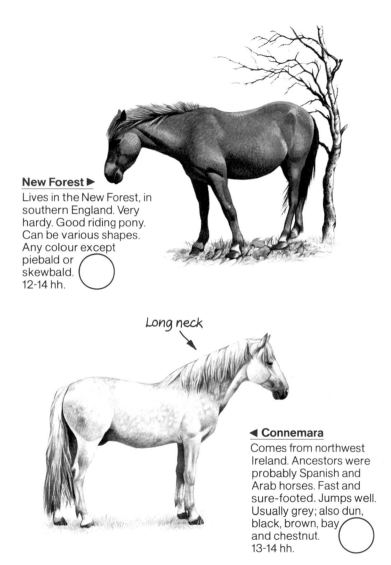

New Forest ▶
Lives in the New Forest, in southern England. Very hardy. Good riding pony. Can be various shapes. Any colour except piebald or skewbald. 12-14 hh.

Long neck

◀ Connemara
Comes from northwest Ireland. Ancestors were probably Spanish and Arab horses. Fast and sure-footed. Jumps well. Usually grey; also dun, black, brown, bay and chestnut. 13-14 hh.

Arab-type head

Tail carried high

Welsh Mountain ▶
Old breed from Wales with
Arab and Thoroughbred
blood. Popular show pony
for riding and driving. Safe
for children. Usually grey
or chestnut; can be any
colour except
piebald or
skewbald.
Up to 12 hh.

Arched
neck

Feather

◀ Welsh Cob
Cross-bred from Welsh
ponies and Andalusian
horses. Strong; a good
trotter. Often driven in
harness. Most colours
except piebald
or skewbald.
14-15 hh.

Heavy head

Flaxen mane and tail

Haflinger ▶
Comes from the Tyrol Mountains, Austria. Very strong and sure-footed. Ideal for forestry work, pulling and carrying loads on steep hillsides. Also ridden, and driven in harness.
Chestnut.
About 14 hh.

Thin neck

Sloping croup

◀ Gotland/Russ
Has lived on the Island of Gotland in Sweden since the Stone Age. Good trotter and jumper. All colours, but often brown, bay or chestnut.
About 13 hh.

Icelandic ▶
Bred from various northern
European ponies. Used as
riding or pack pony.
Some are bred to eat.
Quiet and friendly. Any
colour; often grey, dun,
brown, black or
chestnut.
12-13 hh.

High
knee
action ◀

Mane cut in
crest-like shape ↘

◀ Fjord
Comes from Norway.
Good all purpose worker –
used for riding, driving,
hauling and carrying.
Yellow dun with black
and silver mane
and tail.
13-14.2 hh.

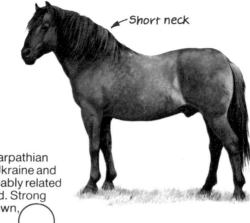

← Short neck

Huçul ▶

Comes from Carpathian
Mountains of Ukraine and
Romania. Probably related
to Tarpan breed. Strong
pack pony. Brown,
dun or bay.
About 13 hh.

◀ Kazakh

Comes from Kazakhstan.
Good long distance
racing pony. Mares' milk
used to make a
fermented drink called
"kumis". Any colour;
often bay, brown
or chestnut.
About 13 hh.

15

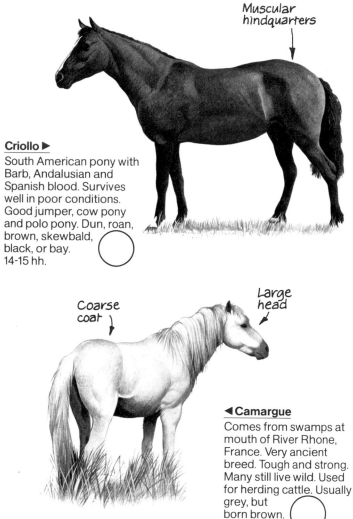

Muscular
hindquarters

Criollo ▶
South American pony with
Barb, Andalusian and
Spanish blood. Survives
well in poor conditions.
Good jumper, cow pony
and polo pony. Dun, roan,
brown, skewbald,
black, or bay.
14-15 hh.

Coarse
coat

Large
head

◀ Camargue
Comes from swamps at
mouth of River Rhone,
France. Very ancient
breed. Tough and strong.
Many still live wild. Used
for herding cattle. Usually
grey, but
born brown.
14-15 hh.

Long, silky coat

Falabella ▶

Comes from Argentina.
A miniature horse;
not very strong. Good
natured; popular
children's pet and
driving pony.
Any colour.
Less than 7 hh.

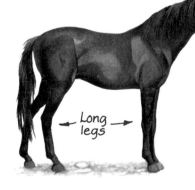

Long legs

◀ Caspian

Wild pony from Iran. Only
about 100 still exist.
Shaped like a miniature
Thoroughbred. Good at
jumping. Usually bay or
brown; also grey. Never
has white
markings.
9.2-11.2 hh.

Coarse mane and coat

Tarpan ▶
Oldest breed in Europe and northern Asia. Was once hunted for food. Two wild herds live in forests in Poland. Very hardy. Usually light brown with black ears, mane, tail, and legs. About 13 hh.

Upright mane

Large head

Thin tail

◀ Przewalski
Also called Asiatic or Mongolian Wild Horse. Unchanged since the Ice Age. Only about 300 exist, some in zoos, others in herds in Gobi Desert, Mongolia. Bay or dun colour. 12-14 hh.

Dark
muzzle

Rounded
body

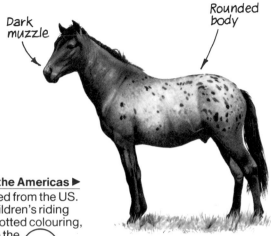

Pony of the Americas ▶
New breed from the US.
Good children's riding
pony. Spotted colouring,
similar to the
Appaloosa.
11.2-13.2 hh.

◀ Sable Island Pony
Comes from Nova Scotia,
Canada. Small and rough.
Lives in wild herds. Feeds
off scrub grass on sand
dunes. Some are sold for
children to ride. All
colours, but often
chestnut.
About 14 hh.

Riding Horses

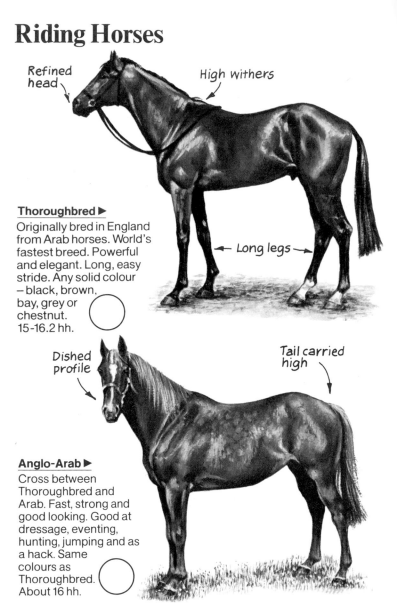

Refined head

High withers

Thoroughbred ▶
Originally bred in England from Arab horses. World's fastest breed. Powerful and elegant. Long, easy stride. Any solid colour – black, brown, bay, grey or chestnut. 15-16.2 hh.

Long legs

Dished profile

Tail carried high

Anglo-Arab ▶
Cross between Thoroughbred and Arab. Fast, strong and good looking. Good at dressage, eventing, hunting, jumping and as a hack. Same colours as Thoroughbred. About 16 hh.

High tail

American Saddlebred ▶
Once used by families in the south of the US as a riding and harness horse. Has three to five ambling gaits (paces). Smooth, effortless ride. Bay, brown or chestnut. 15-15.3 hh.

High knee action

Pinkish muzzle

◀ Appaloosa
North American Indian horse. Cow pony, hunter and jumper. Three main colour types – dark pinkish with lighter back and black spots on loins and hips; white with black spots; bay or black with white spots on hips and loins. 14-15.3 hh.

21

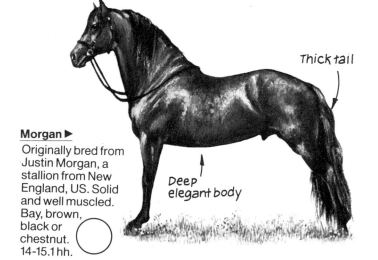

Head nods
with each
step

Long
pasterns

◀ Tennessee Walking Horse

From Tennessee and Louisiana, US. Has three special gaits – flat footed walk; running walk; and running canter. Trots only in harness. Used for riding, driving and farm work. All solid colours. 15-16 hh.

Thick tail

Morgan ▶

Originally bred from Justin Morgan, a stallion from New England, US. Solid and well muscled. Bay, brown, black or chestnut. 14-15.1 hh.

Deep
elegant body

22

Powerful
hindquarters

Quarter Horse ▶
Comes from the
US. Named after
quarter mile races.
Used on ranches as
a cow pony and at
rodeos. Quick and
intelligent.
Any colour.
15-16 hh.

Sloping
croup

Short
neck

◀ Paso Fino
American breed
descended from
horses of Spanish
explorers. Has five
extra gaits. Doesn't
trot. Some do
special, slow "paso
fino" gait.
Any colour.
13-15.2 hh.

23

Thick, arched neck →

Straight profile ↙

◄ Andalusian
Comes from Jerez
region of Spain.
Ancestors were
Barb and Arab horses
and native ponies.
Very sure-footed.
Popular riding horse.
Grey, black,
bay or brown.
15.2-16 hh.

Special tack for bullring ↙

Lusitano ►
Portuguese horse with
same ancestry as
Andalusian. Used by
army; on farms; and in
bull rings. Slightly taller
and lighter build than
Andalusian.
Grey, brown or
bay. 15-16 hh.

Small, fine head with dished profile

Tail carried high

Shagya Arab ▶
A type of Arab from eastern Europe. Can live on little or poor food. Tireless. Popular as a cavalry horse in the First World War. Usually grey. 14-15 hh.

Long back

Large eyes

◀ Polish Arab
Another type of Arab. Bred in Poland since 1500. Used as a racehorse. Very tough and strong. Many exported to England and the US. Can be bay, grey or chestnut. 14.2-15.1 hh.

25

Long neck

Budyonny ▶
From Rostov in Russia.
Can live on poor food.
Once used as a cavalry
horse. Now used for
dressage, racing and
long distance riding.
Brown, black,
bay or chestnut.
About 16 hh.

Upright shoulders

Don ▶
Comes from Don
Valley, Russia.
Once ridden by the
Cossacks. Survives well
in poor grasslands.
Often used as a
carriage horse. Short,
jerky stride.
Always
chestnut.
15-16 hh.

Long
legs

High, narrow body

Akhal-Teke ▶
Ancient breed from
Turkoman Steppes,
Russia. Used for
jumping, racing,
dressage and long
distance riding. Can
stand great heat or
cold. Golden
chestnut, bay, black
or grey.
About
15.1 hh.

Fine coat
with metallic
sheen

Fine, thin
tail

◀ Karabair
Comes from the
mountains of central
Asia. Can work in dry,
hot weather. Fast and
good natured.
Grey, bay
or chestnut.
14.2-15.2 hh.

White mane
and tail

Often has
white face
markings

◀ Palomino
Popular in US.
Descended from
Arab horses.
Classed either as a
breed or a colour.
Most are bred for
shows. Some jump
and hunt. Any shade
of chestnut, with
white mane
and tail.
14-16 hh.

An Overo
may have a
white head

Overo
marking type

Pinto ▶
Bred in US. Used for
riding and herding. Two
marking types: overo–
where most white
areas are below, some
above in an irregular
pattern; tobiano – white,
mostly on back with
some white patches
below in a regular
pattern.
Various
heights.

28

Weak neck

Straight nose

◄ Turkoman
Comes from
Turkoman Steppes,
in northern Iran.
Strong and tireless.
Good riding horse.
Usually grey or bay;
but also dun
or chestnut.
14.3-15.2 hh.

Sloping shoulders

Trakehner ►
Bred mainly in
Poland and
Germany. Works as
a farm and cavalry
horse. Gentle but
brave. Good at
jumping and
dressage. Can be
bay, brown,
black or
chestnut.
16-16.2 hh.

Ram-shaped head

Anglo Norman ▶
Cross-bred in England from big war horses brought over by William the Conqueror. Brave and strong. Good riding and jumping horse. Often chestnut. 15.2-16.3 hh.

◀ Døle/ Gudbrandsaal
Also called Ostland Horse or Dølehest. Comes from Norway. Strong, medium sized horse, once used for pack work. Usually black, brown or bay. About 15 hh.

Lots of feather

Strong
hindquarters

Heavy
shoulders

◄ Hanoverian
German breed
descended from
war horses ridden in
Middle Ages. Strong.
Good show jumper.
Any solid colour;
often bay
or brown.
16-17 hh.

Holstein ►
Bred in marshes of
River Elbe, West
Germany. Big and
strong. Good
carriage horse and
show jumper.
Usually brown,
bay or
black.
16-16.2 hh.

Knabstrup ▶

Danish breed descended from a spotted Spanish mare. Popular as a circus horse. Fast and hardy. Always spotted. Usually white with black spots. About 15 hh.

Short, arched neck

Lipizzaner ▶

Austria's famous breed, used by the Spanish Riding School in Vienna. Bred from Andalusian horses. Excellent dressage horse; also good in harness. Born brown or black, changes to grey. Pure white in old age. 14.3-16 hh.

Barb ▶
Comes from North Africa. There are few pure-bred Barbs left. Can live on poor feed. Fast over short courses. Usually bay, grey, black brown or chestnut. 14-15 hh.

Hard legs and feet

Narrow hindquarters

High withers

◀ Waler
First bred in New South Wales, Australia. Former cavalry horse, now herds cattle on ranches. Also used at rodeos, for show jumping and general riding. Any solid colour. 15-16 hh.

Harness Horses

◀ **Standardbred**
Famous trotting horse from the US. It had to reach a standard speed to become registered, hence the name. Races in carts called sulkies. Any solid colour; usually bay, black, or brown. 15-16 hh.

Long back

Orlov Trotter ▶
Comes from Russia, and named after Count Orlov. Strong and heavy; once used by cavalry. Fairly high knee action. Often grey, also black or bay. 15.2-17 hh.

Some feather

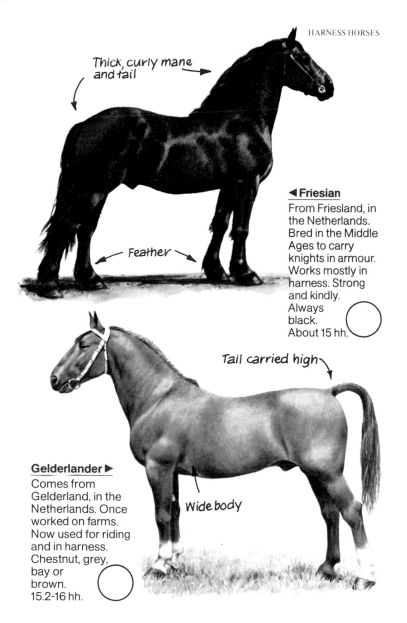

Thick, curly mane and tail

Feather

◀ Friesian
From Friesland, in the Netherlands. Bred in the Middle Ages to carry knights in armour. Works mostly in harness. Strong and kindly. Always black. About 15 hh.

Tail carried high

Gelderlander ▶
Comes from Gelderland, in the Netherlands. Once worked on farms. Now used for riding and in harness. Chestnut, grey, bay or brown. 15.2-16 hh.

Wide body

35

Ram-shaped nose

Heavy neck

◀ **Groningen**
Farm horse from the Netherlands. Heavy but fast. Can live on poor food. Good in harness or for riding. Usually black, bay or brown. 15.2-16 hh.

◀ **Oldenburger**
From northwest Germany. Big and strong; fairly fast. Good trotting and carriage horse. Usually grey, bay, black or brown. 16.2-17.2 hh.

Sloping shoulders

Cleveland Bay ▶
Comes from
Yorkshire, England.
Sure-footed, but not
very fast. Used for
carriage work. Good
jumper. Always bay,
without
white
markings.
15-16.2hh.

High tail   Long back

◀ Hackney
English high-stepping
trotter, famous for its
exaggerated but
graceful action. Used
in light carriages,
for showing.
Bay, black
or brown.
14.3-15.3 hh.

37

Basic type

Kustanair ▶
From Kazakhstan.
Good all purpose
horse. Three kinds:
Steppe – heavy and
slow; Riding – light;
Basic – between the
two (the most
popular). Solid
colours, usually
bay or
chestnut.
15-15.2 hh.

Finnish ▶
Works mainly on
farms and in forests
in Finland. Also used
in trotting races and
for riding. Gentle and
alert. Usually
chestnut. Often has
white
markings.
About 15.2 hh.

Frederiksborg ▶
Old breed from
Denmark. Used
on farms and for
riding. Strong, lively
action. Hard worker.
Usually
chestnut.
Up to 16 hh.

← Short legs →

Roman
nose

Kladruber ▶
From
Czechoslovakia.
First bred by
Emperor Maximilian II
in 16th century. Used
in teams to pull state
coaches, on farms
and in dressage
competitions.
Black or
grey.
16-17 hh.

Small eyes

Nonius ▶
Comes from
Hungary. Named
after Anglo Norman
stallion that founded
the breed. Works on
farms. Black, bay or
brown. Two types:
small – about
15.2 hh;
large –
up to 17 hh.

Light type

◀ Wielkopolski
Popular Polish
breed. Many types:
heavy ones used on
farms; light ones to
drive or ride. Many
bred at state-owned
studs. Usually bay,
brown or
chestnut.
About 16 hh.

Heavy Horses

Short back

Big, round feet

Clydesdale ▶
Comes from Scotland.
Strong and active, but
not too heavy. Popular
on farms. Bay, brown or
black, with white on
feet, face, and
underside.
About 17 hh.

Narrow
head

Shire ▶
Great English heavy
horse. Once carried
knights in armour.
Works on farms. Hard
worker. Usually bay,
black or grey;
lots of white
markings.
Up to 18 hh.

Lots of
feather

Thick neck

Wide chest

◄ Suffolk Punch
Short, stocky breed from Suffolk, England. Does well on little or poor food. Very good natured. Always chestnut. About 16 hh.

◄ Irish Heavy
Good all-purpose farm horse, from Ireland. Makes a top class hunter and jumper if crossed with a Thoroughbred. Often bay; also grey, chestnut or brown. 15.2-16 hh.

Silky coat
(dapple grey)

Percheron ▶
First came from
northern France.
Popular working
horse. Very strong.
Often weighs over a
ton, but needs little
food. Quiet and easy
to handle.
Black or grey.
15.2-17 hh.

Heavy neck
and shoulders

Ardennes ▶
Ancient breed from
France and Belgium.
Once used by
Napoleon's cavalry.
Powerful and gentle.
Can live out in bad
weather. Usually
roan, bay or
chestnut.
About 15.2 hh.

Short head

Dapple grey colour

Boulonnais ▶
Was bred in France for the Crusades. Now works mainly on farms. Strong and good looking. Grey, bay, black or roan. About 16.2 hh.

Breton Heavy ▶
Comes from northwest France. Strong, rugged working horse. Related to Postier Breton (carriage horse). Usually strawberry roan, also bay or chestnut. 15-16 hh.

44

Muscular body

Arched neck

◀ Trait du Nord

Comes from northern France. Breed is increasing; many killed during World War Two. Similar to Ardennes. Quiet and gentle. Usually bay, roan or chestnut. About 16 hh.

◀ Auxois

One of the oldest French breeds. Once used for carriage and farm work. Powerful working horse. Usually bay or strawberry roan. Never black or grey. About 15.2 hh.

45

Heavy neck

Avelignese ►
Bred mainly in
Tuscany, in northern
Italy. Once used as a
pack pony or light
work horse. Short
and muscular. Often
long lived. Usually
chestnut.
About
14.2 hh.

Very deep body

Jutland ►
Danish horse once
used by the Vikings.
Works on farms, and
pulls brewers'
wagons in Denmark.
Often chestnut, but
also roan, black,
grey, bay, or
light brown.
15.2-15.3 hh.

Very
short
legs

◀ Schleswig

Comes from northern Germany. Once used to carry knights in armour. Now used mostly on farms, and for hauling. Nearly always chestnut. 15.2-16 hh.

Short legs

◀ Pinzgauer Noriker

Oldest Austrian breed. May be descended from a Roman breed. Quiet and strong. Good for pulling ploughs. Bay, chestnut or spotted. 15-16 hh.

High, arched neck

Vladimir ▶
Strong, active
horse from Vladimir, in
Russia. Used for
heavy and light
harness work.
Bay, roan,
or chestnut.
About 16 hh.

Short neck

Heavy, muscular body

Dutch Heavy ▶
Ancient, very pure
breed. Bred from
Belgian horses.
Popular on farms in
the Netherlands,
where it has its own
show. Very strong
and heavy. Bay, grey
or chestnut.
Up to
16.3 hh.

48

Parts of the Horse

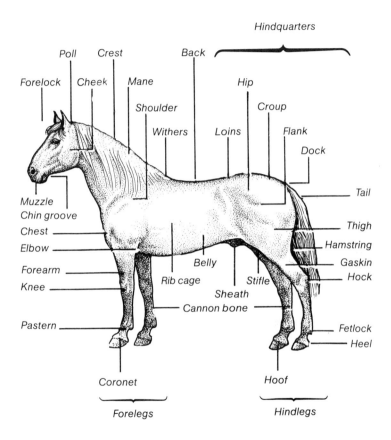

Hindquarters

Poll Crest Back

Forelock Cheek Mane Hip

Shoulder Croup

Withers Loins Flank

Dock

Muzzle Tail
Chin groove
Chest Thigh
Elbow Hamstring
Forearm Gaskin
Knee Belly Hock
Rib cage Stifle
Sheath
Cannon bone
Pastern Fetlock
Heel

Coronet Hoof

Forelegs Hindlegs

Looking after a pony

Keeping a pony in a field

In the wild, ponies live in herds; they move around a great deal, grazing and drinking, and rest for only a few hours at night. There are many things they miss in captivity. If you keep your pony in a field, try to give it:

● Other horses or ponies to keep it company.

● Good grazing. Each pony needs at least one acre of good grass. You may need to change fields in spring or autumn, to let the grass grow again. Pick up droppings to stop worms from spreading.

● Plenty of fresh water to drink.

● Shelter. Trees, a thick hedge or a shed. Keep a salt or mineral block in the shed.

● Strong fencing. A post and rail wood fence is best. Wire is all right if it is tightly secured to strong posts with the bottom wire 45cm (18") from the ground.

Thick hedge or shed for shelter

Constant supply of fresh water

Other horses or ponies for company

Strong post and rail fence

50

Keeping a pony in a stable

It isn't natural for ponies to live indoors. If you keep your pony in a stable, it will need special care. You must do the following things:

● Exercise your pony every day. Ride it for at least one hour, or turn it out in a field for a few hours.

● Give it the right kind of food. A pony needs plenty of bulk food, like hay, to nibble during the day and night. It also needs short food, like corn, in small amounts, in the morning, at night, and perhaps at midday.

● Make sure it always has plenty of fresh water.

Stable equipment

Skip   Pitchfork   Brush   Barrow   Spade   Fork

● Muck (clean) out the stable every morning. Clean out wet straw and droppings to stop bad smells and foot disease. Add fresh bedding of straw, wood shavings, peat or sawdust. The bed must be thick enough to keep the pony warm and stop it from hurting itself. Pick up droppings at night.

● Groom your pony every day. This will keep its coat clean and its skin healthy.

Jute rug

● Keep your pony warm in winter. If it has a full coat, a jute rug will be enough. If it has been clipped, it will need blankets under the rug too.

● Let fresh air into the stable to stop your pony from getting coughs and colds. Leave the top door open unless it is bitterly cold. It is best if the window and door on opposite sides of the stable are not both open together.

If you want to alter your pony's feeding or exercise pattern, do it gradually. Ponies need time to get used to new routines.

Leave top door open

Feeding

What a pony eats

In its natural environment, a pony eats small amounts of bulk food (mostly grass) almost continually throughout the day. A pony kept in a stable eats hay instead of grass. The best type of hay to feed your pony is meadow or mixture hay.

If you keep your pony in a field, it may need no extra food during the summer, providing there is plenty of good grass. During the winter, when the grass has stopped growing and is very poor, your pony may need up to 6kg (13lbs) of hay a day, and even more in frosty or snowy weather.

As well as grass or hay, a pony may need high protein "short" feeds. These are a mixture of corn or cubes and a bulk food like bran or chaff.

You can use these foods to make up a short feed for you pony:

- Corn – Oats or barley. Use crushed or split oats rather than whole oats. Don't give oats to small or excitable ponies. Barley is more fattening but has less food value than oats. Use either crushed barley, or whole barley boiled for two to three hours.

- Cubes – Animal feed stores sell different kinds of cubes (also called "nuts"). Read the feeding instructions on the sack carefully.

- Bran – Mix bran into a feed with corn or cubes. It will make your pony eat more slowly and digest its foot better.

- Chaff – Chopped hay. Use chaff in the same way as bran.

- Flaked maize – A rich and fairly fattening food, unsuitable for small ponies.

- Sugar beet – good for fattening ponies up. Soak it in water for 24 hours before feeding.

- Linseed – Occasionally give your pony small amounts of boiled linseed; it has good food value and will improve your pony's coat.

- Vegetables – If there is no grass, give your pony fresh root vegetables, or green leaves like sprouts or cabbage leaves. Slice carrots, turnips, parsnips, or other root vegetables lengthwise before adding them to the feed.

Remember to leave a salt or mineral lick (block) in your pony's field or stable.

Haynet

▲ Put hay in a rack or haynet to prevent it from being wasted.

▲ Put short feeds in a manger or galvanized bin.

How to feed a pony

These are the basic rules for feeding a pony:

- Make sure your pony always has enough grass or hay to eat.
- Feed your pony little and often. Ponies have small stomachs, so they can't digest large meals properly.
- Give your pony water to drink before, not after you feed it.
- Never ride your pony right after a feed; wait about an hour.
- Feed your pony at the same time every day.

Each pony will need different amounts of different kinds of food. What you feed your pony will depend on its temperament, size and health, how much work it has to do, the time of year, where the pony is kept, how much good grass is available, and how much the pony has to eat to keep its weight up.

The table below will give you an idea of what you might feed an average 14 hh pony in one day, at different times of the year.

Table showing approximate daily feeds for an average 14 hh pony				
SEASON	Summer	Summer	Winter	Winter
WHERE KEPT	Field	Field	Stable	Stable
WORK	Light riding	Daily training and shows	Light riding	Daily exercise and hunting
EARLY MORNING		1 kg (2 lb) cubes (if the pony is worked very hard)	3 kg (6 lbs) hay	2 kg (4 lbs) hay, ½ kg (1 lb) oats, ½ kg (1 lb) cubes, ½–1 kg (1–2 lbs) bran or chaff dampened with water
MID-DAY				2 kg (4½ lbs) hay, ½ kg (1 lb) oats, ½ kg (1 lb) cubes, ½–1 kg (1–2 lbs) bran or chaff dampened with water
EVENING	½–1 kg (1–2 lb) cubes (if there is too little good grass)	1–1½ kg (2–3 lbs) oats, ½–1 kg (1–2 lbs) bran or chaff dampened with water	2 kg (4½ lbs) hay, 1–2 kg (2–4½ lbs) oats, ½–1 kg (1–2 lbs) bran or chaff ¼ kg (½ lb) sugar beet (weigh before soaking) ½–1 kg (1–2 lbs) fresh vegetables	2 kg (4½ lbs) hay, ½–1 kg (1–2 lbs) oats, ¼ kg (½ lb) flaked maize. ¼ kg (½ lb) sugar beet (weigh before soaking), ½–1 kg (1–2 lbs) fresh vegetables

Grooming

You must groom your pony every day if it is kept in a stable.

Pick out its feet with a hoof pick, pulling the pick from heel to toe.

If your pony has a full coat, brush off dirt and stains with a dandy brush, working back from the top of its neck. Always brush in the direction the coat lies.

Next, clean its skin and coat with the body brush. This brush has short, soft hairs. Clean the brush by pulling it across a metal or rubber currycomb. Brush the pony's head with the body brush, too, taking great care to be gentle. The body brush is also used to brush its mane and tail. If you comb its mane with a mane comb, do it carefully, as it will break hairs very easily.

Clean its eyes, nostrils and dock with a damp sponge.

Brush around and under its hooves with hoof oil.

Wipe it all over with a clean cloth to make its coat gleam; as a finishing touch, smooth down its mane and tail with a damp brush.

Hoof pick

Dandy brush

Body brush

Metal currycomb

Rubber currycomb

Mane comb

Hoof oil and brush

Sponge and bucket

Cloth

Shoeing

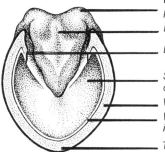

Parts of the hoof

Heel – Back of hoof

Frog – Acts as a cushion

Bars – Where the wall turns in

Sole – Guards the foot, but can become bruised

Wall – Nail-like, no feeling

White line – Between feeling and insensitive parts of hoof

Toe – Front of hoof

Most working horses and ponies need to wear metal horseshoes, to stop their feet from getting worn down. Shoes also stop the hoof from becoming cracked, bruised or out of shape.

If your pony works a lot, it will need new shoes every six weeks. In that time, the shoes may wear smooth, and the pony's feet will grow out of them.

Horseshoes must be made to fit properly. The blacksmith or farrier takes the old shoe off first. Then he trims down the wall of the hoof, and fits a new shoe. He can make it fit better if it is hot and pliable. The shoe is nailed to the wall of the hoof where it won't hurt the pony. Finally, the blacksmith files the surface of the shoe smooth.

Riding

A horse has to be carefully prepared before it is ready to be ridden. This is known as "breaking" and "schooling". The horse has to get used to having a rider on its back, and must learn to obey commands. A horse can be broken for riding when it is three years old, and will have an active life until it is 20, if well cared for. (Horses normally live for 25 to 30 years.)

A rider has just as much to learn as a horse does. He must learn to sit so that the horse is well-balanced and can move freely. He must also learn to give the horse signals it can understand.

If you want to learn to ride, find a riding school that is approved by horse associations, so you can be sure your teacher is a good one. You should be given a quiet, well-schooled horse or pony to begin on.

These are the aids a rider uses to control his horse:

Hands – These hold the reins which control the bit. The bit lies on a sensitive part of the horse's jaw, so keep a steady but gentle contact with the bit. Use your hands to slow your horse down, and to turn it to the right and left.

Legs – Use your lower leg and heel to make your horse move forward, and turn properly (bending its spine). Your legs should be close to the horse's body. Your heels should be pushed down. If the horse moves suddenly, keep your balance by gripping the saddle with your

Wear a hard hat

Look ahead

Straight back

Hands just above withers

Elbows in

Legs close to horse's body

Heels down

thighs and knees.

Body – Body weight can be used to drive the horse forward. If you want to slow down, let your weight sink into the saddle. Tilting your body slightly to one side can help you change your horse's balance. This is useful for changing direction at the canter.

Voice – Horses have very sharp hearing, and can learn to recognize many sounds. To encourage your horse to move forward if it hesitates, click your tongue. A slow, quiet "Whoa . . ." will steady it down. Never scream or shout near a horse. This will frighten it and it may bolt.

Tack

Good tack (saddles and bridles) is very important. A plain snaffle bridle is best for most ponies. Fit the bridle carefully; ask someone to help you adjust it to fit your pony if you aren't sure how to do it.

For ordinary riding, a general purpose saddle is best. The saddle sits on the pony's back, just behind the withers; it should be well clear of the pony's spine at all times.

Tack is made of leather. You should clean your tack every time you use it, to prevent it from becoming hard, and cracking. Clean it with a damp sponge first, then saddle soap it to keep it soft.

General purpose saddle

Snaffle bridle

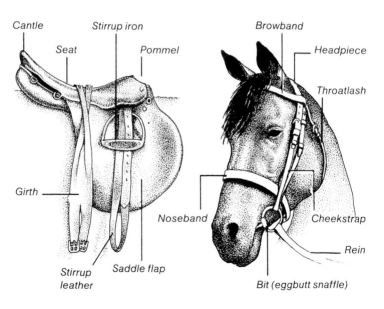

General purpose saddle — Cantle, Stirrup iron, Seat, Pommel, Girth, Stirrup leather, Saddle flap

Snaffle bridle — Browband, Headpiece, Throatlash, Noseband, Cheekstrap, Rein, Bit (eggbutt snaffle)

Glossary

All purpose – horse or pony that is good at different things, like jumping, hunting and gymkhana games.

Cob – short, stocky horse (not more than 15.3 hh). Quiet and well-behaved.

Colt - male horse up to three years old.

Dressage – the training of a horse. It includes breaking and basic schooling, as well as the more difficult precision movements that are performed by well-schooled, obedient horses.

Event horse - used in horse trials, which include dressage, show jumping and cross-country riding.

Filly - female horse up to three years old.

Flat racing - racing over short courses without jumps.

Foal - male or female horse up to one year old.

Gelding – male horse that has been neutered.

Gymkhana - show where mounted games, like bending and sack races, are held.

Hack – well-behaved, well-schooled riding horse of light build. Some women ride hacks side-saddle.

Hunter - horse that can gallop cross-country and jump well. It must be strong and very fit.

Hurdler – horse that races and jumps hurdles, usually over courses about four kilometres (2½ miles) long.

Mare - female horse more than three years old.

Point-to-point - amateur jumping races. They used to be run from one church steeple (point) to the next.

In this gymkhana race, riders lose points if they spill water

School master – old, well-behaved, well-schooled horse or pony. Safe and reliable for people learning to ride.

Show jumping – jumping competitions.

Show horse/pony – competes at shows in various classes, like "Working Hunter" or "Children's Riding Pony". Judged on its appearance, schooling and suitability for the class entered.

Stallion – male horse more than three years old. Usually kept only for breeding.

Steeplechase – race run over fences on courses about eight kilometres (five miles) long.

Trotter – horse or pony that races in harness; it may either trot or "pace" (move the fore and hind legs on each side together).

Hunter

Mare and foal

Riding opportunities

There are various kinds of riding opportunities; learning special skills, like show jumping or dressage, and catering for those who just want to go trekking in the country. Before you try anything you should have several one-hour riding lessons. You can find out about kinds of riding from horse magazines. Try to pick one that is approved by a horse association.

Some riding schools run courses lasting anything from a couple of days to a few weeks. The pupils usually stay in lodgings near the school. If you go on one of these courses, you may have lessons in the morning, and relax in the afternoon, often with gymkhana games. Branches of the Pony Club run summer camps lasting about a week. At camp, you will learn more about riding, jumping and pony care. The camp may finish off with a small show or gymkhana. If you don't own a pony, you may be able to hire one from a riding stable for a week.

Pony trekking

You don't need a great deal of experience it you want to go pony trekking. You will be given a pony to ride, and you will have to feed and groom it yourself. You will go on a longer ride every day, finishing up with a whole day's ride on the last day of your stay.

Pony Club camp

Clubs to join

UK

The best club to join is the *Pony Club*, which is part of the *British Horse Society*; both are based at the National Equestrian Centre, Stoneleigh, Kenilworth, Warwickshire.

US

United States Pony Clubs, 893 5, Matlack St., West Chester, PA 19382-4913.

Useful addresses

UK

Association of British Riding Schools, Chesham House, 56 Green End Road, Sawtry, Huntingdon.
British Driving Society, 10 Marley Avenue, New Milton, Hampshire.
British Show Pony Society, Smale Farm, Wisborough Green, Billingshurst, Sussex.
British Veterinary Society, 7 Mansfield Street, Portland Place, London W1.

US

The National Horseman, P.O. Box 43397, Louisville, Ky 40253.
National Steeplechase & Hunt, P.O. Box 308, Elmont, NY 11003.
American Horse Show Assoc., 598 Madison Avenue, New York, NY 10022.
National Horse and Pony Youth Activities Council, 929 South Fourth Street, Louisville, KY 40203.

Books to read

UK

The Manual of Horsemanship. (British Horse Society). A must.
Keeping a Pony at Grass. (Pony Club). Lots of practical advice.
Children's Encyclopedia of Horses & Ponies. C. Rawson, J. Spector, E. Poling (Usborne). Illustrated international guide.
Summerhays' Encyclopaedia for Horsemen. (Frederick Warne). Old and respected reference book; has been updated.
The Encyclopedia of the Horse. (Ebury Press/Pelham). Large, detailed and fairly expensive.
Feeding Ponies. W. Miller (J. A. Allen & Co.).
Horses and Riding. B. Skelton (Stanley Paul). Packed with first-class advice and ideas.

US

The Horse Owner's Handbook. Lloyd S. McKibbin, D.V.M. (W. B. Saunders Co.). An excellent reference book about injuries and illnesses in the horse.
Riding from A to Z. Peter Churchill (Taplinger Publishing Co.). A solid, practical horse guide.
The Classic World of Horses, by Robert Magee (Arco Publishing). An illustrated reference covering several aspects of the sport.
Western Horse Behavior and Training, by Robert W. Miller (Double-Day and Co., Inc.). A detailed reference for training.
The Light Horse Breeds, by John W. Patten (A.S. Barnes & Co., Inc.). An informative and historical reference.

Checklist

The horses and ponies on this checklist are arranged in alphabetical order. When you see one, write down the date in the blank space next to each name and where you saw it – at a horse show, for instance.

	Date seen	Where seen		Date seen	Where seen
Akhal-Teke			Dartmoor		
American Saddlebred			Døle		
Andalusian			Don		
Anglo-Arab			Dutch Heavy		
Anglo Norman			Exmoor		
Appaloosa			Falabella		
Arab (any type)			Fell		
Ardennes			Finnish		
Auxois			Fjord		
Avelignese			Fredericksborg		
Barb			Friesian		
Boulonnais			Gelderlander		
Breton			Gotland		
Budyonny			Groningen		
Camargue			Hackney		
Caspian			Haflinger		
Cleveland Bay			Hanoverian		
Clydesdale			Highland		
Connemara			Holstein		
Criollo			Huçul		
Dale			Icelandic		

	Date seen	Where seen		Date seen	Where seen
Irish Heavy			Shire		
Jutland			Standardbred		
Karabair			Suffolk Punch		
Kazakh			Tarpan		
Kladruber			Tennesee Walking Horse		
Knabstrup			Thoroughbred		
Kustanair			Trait du Nord		
Lipizzaner			Trakehner		
Lusitano			Turkoman		
Morgan			Vladimir		
New Forest			Waler		
Nonius			Welsh Cob		
Oldenburger			Welsh Mountain		
Orlov Trotter			Wielkopolski		
Palomino					
Paso Fino					
Percheron					
Pinto					
Pinzgauer Noriker					
Pony of the Americas					
Przewalski					
Quarter Horse					
Sable Island					
Schleswig					
Shetland					

Index